MISCHIEF ON THE MOORS

STEPHEN DAVIES

Illustrated by MARTA DORADO

BLOOMSBURY EDUCATION

LONDON   OXFORD   NEW YORK   NEW DELHI   SYDNEY

BLOOMSBURY EDUCATION

Bloomsbury Publishing Plc
50 Bedford Square, London, WC1B 3DP, UK
29 Earlsfort Terrace, Dublin 2, Ireland

BLOOMSBURY, BLOOMSBURY EDUCATION and the Diana logo are trademarks of
Bloomsbury Publishing Plc

First published in Great Britain in 2023 by Bloomsbury Publishing Plc

A catalogue record for this book is available from the British Library

ISBN: PB: 9781801991780; ePDF: 9781801991766; ePub: 9781801991759

2 4 6 8 10 9 7 5 3 1

Text design by Laura Neate

Printed and bound in in the UK by CPI Group Ltd, CR0 4YY

FSC
MIX
Paper | Supporting
responsible forestry
FSC® C171272
www.fsc.org

To find out more about our authors and books visit www.bloomsbury.com and sign up
for our newsletters

MISCHIEF ON THE MOORS

CONTENTS

CHAPTER 1

It was home time at Alsington Primary School. Daisy Wright ran to her BMX, crammed her school bag into the bike basket and pedalled hard out of the school gates.

"Wait for me!" Her older sister Libby was on her own bike, straining to catch up. "You're only allowed to ride home if I'm with you, remember?"

"It's not my fault if you can't keep up!" crowed Daisy, pedalling past a

row of thatched cottages and out of
the village.

Like most lanes in Devon, this one
had high hedgerows on either side,
which occasionally arched over to
form a green tunnel. At some points,
the lane was so narrow that Daisy
could stretch her arms out wide and
feel the hawthorn leaves rushing past
on both sides, tickling her palms.

"Put your hands back on the
handlebars!" called Libby.

"You're so far behind, I can't hear
you!" Daisy laughed.

The sisters rode through the
chocolate box villages of Smokey

Cross and Pinchaford, then up onto the open moor.

Daisy and Liberty Wright had lived on Dartmoor all their lives. Their school friends in Alsington often teased them that they lived in the middle of nowhere, but Daisy and Libby didn't mind. They loved the moorland with its bright green bracken, its yellow flowers and its vast swathes of purple heather. They loved their cottage in Manaton with its dolls-house windows peeking out from under a thatched roof. They even loved the long bike journey to and from school. The views over Hound Tor Marshes were stunning and Haytor Quarry was on their route.

Nature's Stunt Bowl. That was what Libby and Daisy called the quarry. Every afternoon they would balance on the top edge with their knobbly front wheels poking out over nothingness, and feel that dizzying stomach-lurch as they dropped in. The quarry had flat areas for nollies, grassy inclines for fakies, and rocky slopes steep enough for any amount of airtime. Best of all, it was abandoned. They had the quarry all to themselves, any time they wanted.

"You first," said Libby, as they arrived at the top edge.

Daisy took a deep breath and jerked her BMX forward into thin air.

Her tummy dropped away and she accelerated down the granite ramp into the quarry. Libby followed, and the sisters crisscrossed the stunt bowl to and fro with wild shrieks of abandon.

After half an hour, they lay side by side on a flat rock, bruised and happy. They stared up at the clouds and let their breathing return to normal.

"Only two sleeps till the fête," said Libby.

Daisy grinned. The Manaton fête always took place on the first Saturday of May, and it was the highlight of their social calendar. Dad always called it 'the fête worse than death' but secretly he loved it as much as the rest of the family. There would be Morris dancers, a dog show and competitions galore.

"I can't wait," said Daisy. "I've decided to enter the Garden on a Dinner Plate competition, the Flower Arrangement in a Thimble competition and the Miniature Scarecrow competition."

Libby laughed. "They should replace all of those with a single competition called the Make Something Tiny competition."

Daisy got to her feet and picked up her BMX. "I'll collect some heather for my thimble while I'm here," she said. "Are you coming?"

The sisters rode up the steep bridleway to the foot of Haytor Rocks, two colossal granite formations overlooking eastern Dartmoor. They collected some sprigs of purple heather, then headed home to Manaton.

At least, they thought they were heading to Manaton. Mysteriously, after ten minutes of pedalling, they found themselves right back at Haytor Rocks.

"That was weird," said Libby, and they set off again.

The Manaton bridleway led them down into a waterlogged hollow, up onto a wind-buffeted ridge, straight ahead for what seemed like miles, and all the way back to Haytor Rocks.

"What's going on?" said Daisy. "We know where we are, and yet for some reason..."

Her voice trailed off into silence. This was impossible. They had known and loved this part of Dartmoor all their lives. They had hiked and camped all over Haytor Vale. They had done stunt riding, letterboxing, orienteering…

Orienteering! Daisy rummaged in her bag and pulled out her old orienteering compass. She carried it for emergencies, in case the famous Dartmoor fog descended, as occasionally it did.

"Good thinking," said Libby, craning her neck to look at the compass.

The compass needle was spinning round and round, as if trying to decide which way was north. The sisters stared at it in horror.

"Libby?" said Daisy in a small voice. "Libby, I'm scared."

CHAPTER 2

A blanket of green-tinged fog
descended over the moors, and Daisy
felt a sudden chill in her bones.

"We need to get out of here, fast,"
said Libby. "I wish my brain wasn't so
addled right now."

Addled. The word reminded Daisy
of a line from one of Gran's favourite
Dartmoor poems. Gran had lived with
them for the last two years before
she died. Daisy always pictured her

surrounded by her large collection of books and her even larger collection of teapots.

How did Gran's poem go again? *With addled mind and weary legs, yon traveller be pixie led...*

"Libby, I know what's happening!" shouted Daisy. "We're being pixie led!"

Gran and her friends all used to believe the Dartmoor legends about travellers getting disoriented by mischievous pixies. Most of these tales included the same peculiar secret to breaking the spell.

"Quick!" cried Libby. "Turn your coat inside out."

As soon as the girls reversed their coats, the fog began to swirl and clear. There in front of them was Bowerman's Nose, a tall rock overlooking Manaton.

The brain fog cleared as well. Clear-eyed and clear-headed, the sisters cycled home.

"Mum! Dad!" cried Libby, bursting into Dove Cottage. "Guess who just got pixie led!"

Their parents were in the kitchen, preparing for the village fête. Mum was sorting through a basket of carrots on the table, while Dad was hopping to and fro, trying to unscrew the lid from a jar of pickled beetroot. He had clearly been struggling for a while,

because his cheeks were the same colour as the beetroot in the jar.

"We were totally lost!" cried Daisy. "We had to turn our coats inside out to find our way home."

"That's nice." Mum held up three spindly carrots. "Tell me, girls, are these three the same size?"

Libby and Daisy looked at each other, then at the carrots. Like most children in Manaton, they found it hard to get their parents' attention during the run-up to the village fête.

"Pretty much," said Daisy.

"'Pretty much' butters no parsnips," said Mum, who had inherited many of Gran's peculiar Devonshire sayings.

"Or in this case, carrots," quipped Dad, still wrestling with the jar lid. "Your mum is entering the Three Identical Carrots competition at the village fête, and the judges are very strict about the 'identical' bit. As for the Best Pickled Beetroot competition, we definitely won't win a rosette if I can't open the jar."

Libby took the beetroot jar from Dad, carried it to the sink and began to run the lid under hot water. Meanwhile, Daisy helped Mum search the basket for three equally proportioned carrots.

"Look at this one." Mum held up a carrot with a bite already taken out of it. "We really should hire a professional to sort out our mole problem."

"I saw a 'No More Moles' flyer on the noticeboard outside church the other day," said Libby.

"Did you?" Mum's face brightened. "Be a star and nip down there now, would you? I really need that telephone number."

Libby rolled her eyes but she did not argue. She handed the warm beetroot jar back to Dad and went to fetch her BMX.

As Daisy left the kitchen and went upstairs, she heard a soft pop and a cheer of triumph from Dad. "No lid too tight for Mr Wright!" he sang at the top of his voice.

Alone at last, Daisy's mind returned to pixies. She had never taken the legends seriously before today, but now she was eager to find out as much as possible.

She dragged her bedside table onto the landing and stood on it to release the trapdoor leading to the loft. A stepladder slid down from above and Daisy climbed up, rung by rung.

The crawl space under the thatched roof was a mess of dry wheat and cobwebs, dimly lit by one electric bulb. Daisy edged forward, trying to avoid being scraped by the sharp ends of the hazelwood roof spurs.

A row of cardboard boxes stood along a wooden board on the far side of the loft. Daisy opened the first one and peered inside.

Teapots.

She tried another box.

More teapots.

Daisy tried a third box, and this
time she struck lucky. It was full of
Gran's old books, and halfway down
was the book she had been searching

for: *Tales of the Dartmoor Pixies* by Eileen Williams. Daisy opened it at random and began to read.

Relations between pixies and humans are never straightforward. Dartmoor pixies often play tricks on people or lead them astray on the moors. But treat a pixie kindly by giving it food, water or a shiny trinket, and it might repay you by harvesting your corn at night or by turning your milk into butter.

CHAPTER 3

After school on Friday, Libby and
Daisy collected their BMXs, crammed
their bags into the baskets and
pedalled out of the school gates faster
than ever.

"Girls!" Miss Handforth was
gesturing at them from the playground.
"Your coats are inside out!"

"It's all right, Miss!" Libby called
back over her shoulder. "We like them
that way!"

The girls cycled all the way to Haytor without stopping. As soon as they reached the granite outcrop, they jumped off their bikes and unzipped their bags.

Libby took out an enamel bowl, filled it from her school water bottle and laid it on a flat rock at the foot of the tor. "Here, pixies!" she called. "Come and drink!"

Daisy delved in her own bag and pulled out a cheap, glittery ring that she had won in a Christmas cracker two years ago, along with a limp fish finger she had saved from lunch. She laid the gifts beside the bowl of water and sat down next to her sister, with her back against the tor.

Minutes passed, then Daisy felt a slight vibration through her spine. She turned and pressed her ear to the rock… and that was when she heard it.

"Hey! Hey! Hey!" The sound of music and happy chanting was faint but clear, rising up from deep below the tor.

Libby put her ear to the rock, too, her jaw dropping open in astonishment. "Pixies," she mouthed silently.

Daisy took *Tales of the Dartmoor Pixies* out of her bag and opened it to the first page, a detailed map of Dartmoor.

"Look," she said. "In the olden days, when this book was made, Haytor used to be spelled Hey with an 'e'."

"Are you thinking what I'm thinking?" Libby's eyes shone. "I reckon that people in Gran's generation heard the pixies partying here, and they named the place after the sound!"

The girls stayed on the moor for a long time, their ears pressed to the granite. The shadow of the tor lengthened and shifted, and the breeze turned cold.

"We should go," said Libby.

They put their bags back in their baskets, and fastened their bike helmets. Before they set off, Daisy took one last look at the rock.

"Libby!" she cried.

The ring and the fish finger were nowhere to be seen, and the water bowl was completely empty.

The girls rode hard all the way home, eager to tell their parents what they had seen and heard. As they pushed their bikes into the back garden of Dove Cottage, they noticed Dad's feet poking out from behind the runner beans.

"Hey, Dad!" panted Libby, putting her bike back in the shed. "You'll never guess what happened this afternoon. We heard an underground pixie party at Haytor!"

"And they took the gifts we left for them," Daisy added excitedly. "If that's not proof that Dartmoor pixies exist, I don't know what is!"

A man crawled out from the carrot patch. Libby and Daisy squealed in shock.

It was not Dad. It was a complete stranger with pale blue eyes and a straggly beard.

"How interesting." The man's voice was as smooth as a millpond. "Where exactly on Haytor did this happen? The tall rock to the west or the wider formation to the east?"

The girls did not answer. They edged past the man and hurried into the kitchen.

"Mum," said Libby, closing the door behind her, "there's a strange man in the carrot patch."

Mum looked up from her laptop. "That's Mr Butchart from No More Moles, dear. He's sorting out our mole problem."

After dinner that evening, Daisy worked on her entries for the village fête, but her mind was hopelessly distracted by the afternoon's excitement. Her Garden on a Dinner Plate was a mess, her Flowers in a Thimble refused to stand upright, and the Miniature Scarecrow remained a shapeless fistful of straw, however long she worked on it.

By eight thirty, Daisy could no longer bear the sight of her disastrous projects. "I'm going to bed," she said out loud.

CHAPTER 4

That night, Daisy dreamed of pixies. Dressed in green and brown rags, they harvested wheat, made butter and danced in secret caverns beneath the marshy moors.

Early on Saturday morning, just as Daisy was surfacing from her pixie dreams, the handle of her bedroom door turned silently. Somebody crept across the carpet and flung the curtains wide, flooding the room with morning sun.

"Wake up, lazybones!" cried Dad. "Prepare yourself for a fête worse than death!"

Daisy groaned and pulled the duvet over her head.

"That's odd," said Dad. "There seems to be a Dartmoor pony in our garden!" He stared for a while, then sprinted out of the room and down the stairs.

Daisy got up and went to the window. Dad was right. A sturdy, brown pony stood in the middle of the vegetable patch, munching on a runner bean. Its flanks were slick with sweat and the edge of its black mane was crusted with salt. Somebody had ridden this pony during the night, and ridden it hard.

Dad appeared in the garden below, still wearing his dressing gown and slippers. He opened the back gate and began to circle the pony, waving and shoo-ing.

Daisy watched him, deep in thought. Dartmoor ponies lived wild on the moors, and they were so skittish that no one could get near them, let alone ride them. And yet this pony had not only been ridden, it had been made to jump the wall as well.

Libby shuffled into Daisy's bedroom. She wiped the sleep out of her eyes and goggled at Daisy's desk.

"Daisy, they're amazing!" Libby gushed. "I didn't know I had such a talented sister!"

Daisy looked. Her shoddy craft efforts from the previous night had been replaced by three glorious displays.

A gorgeous miniature garden sat on a rose-rimmed dinner plate, complete with heather, lichen and delicate butterfly orchids. A beautiful arrangement of daisies, bluebells and cowslips nestled in Gran's silver thimble and, standing behind it, a stunningly detailed scarecrow leered out from under a straw hat. The scarecrow was about thirty centimetres tall, with tiny tufts of straw poking from its shirt sleeves and trouser legs.

"Please let me team up with you at the fête today," Libby pleaded. "I won't pretend I helped you. I just want to stand beside you when they give you all three rosettes!"

Daisy reached out and took her sister's hand. "I didn't make any of this," she whispered. "It must have been the pixies. They didn't find any milk to churn or wheat to harvest, so they helped us with our competition entries instead!"

That morning, the Wright household was abuzz with activity. Libby and Daisy got dressed, gulped down some cereal and helped their parents load the car with the various competition entries: carrots, beetroot, coffee and walnut cake, mini-garden, flower thimble and mini-scarecrow. There was so much stuff to transport, there was hardly any room in the back seat for the girls.

"You two go ahead on your bikes," said Mum. "We'll see you at the fête, okay?"

Libby and Daisy raced each other down the hill towards the village green, where the square tower of St Winifred's church poked up above the trees.

When they got to the fête, they completely lost track of time, bouncing from one activity to the next. They got their faces painted, they guessed the number of balloons in the cabin of Farmer

Seb's tractor, they hooked plastic ducks in a paddling pool, and they cheered and clapped wildly at the dog agility display.

At precisely eleven o'clock, the vicar's voice came over the loud speaker, inviting children to bring their Garden on a Dinner Plate entries to the tea tent. Daisy and Libby ran to the car park, but their car was nowhere to be seen.

"Where are Mum and Dad with all our stuff?" cried Daisy. "We're going to miss the competition!"

A magnificent English oak tree loomed over the car park, almost as high as the tower of St Winifred's. Libby ran to the oak tree and swung herself up into the lower branches. The tree was bursting into leaf, as it did every May. Hundreds of yellow catkins caressed Libby's face as she clambered up.

"Any sign of them?" shouted Daisy.

Libby brushed aside the bough in front of her and looked out over the village and the moors beyond. "I can see the car!" she called. "It's in the field next to our house. It's driving around in circles!"

"Oh no!" Daisy grabbed her BMX from the bike rack. "They're being pixie led!"

She zoomed off towards the field, standing up on her pedals for extra speed and power. It took her ten minutes to catch up with Mum and Dad, and another ten to escort them to the village fête. They arrived with goofy, embarrassed expressions on their faces – and their fleecy jackets turned inside out.

"Who would have thought it?" said Mum, getting out of the car. "Enchanted by pixies in this day and age! They could have led us right into the Hound Tor Marshes if they'd wanted to, and then what would have become of us?"

"You've missed the dinner plate and thimble competitions," Libby told her sister. "But if you're fast, you can still enter the Miniature Scarecrow competition."

The girls rushed into the tea tent, where a dozen mini-scarecrows were lined up on a long trestle table. Daisy added her scarecrow on the end, and waited for the judges to make their way along the line.

Just outside the tea tent was the Whack-a-Mole stand, manned by Mr Butchart. He was surrounded by 'moles' – black, straw-stuffed socks with beady eyes – and in front of him was a long, sloping tube and a mallet.

"Roll up, roll up!" Mr Butchart kept calling. "Three whacks for a pound."

The judges arrived at Daisy's scarecrow. One of the judges was

Farmer Seb, a stocky man with a sunburned nose. The other was the tall figure of Reverend Sykes, vicar of St Winifred's.

"My word!" said the vicar, peering over the top of his glasses. "How splendidly ugly."

"Speak for yourself!" retorted a little voice.

The vicar frowned at Daisy. "Did you say something, girl?"

"No." Daisy's cheeks burned with embarrassment.

"'Tis a proper job, that one," grinned Farmer Seb, admiring the scarecrow. "There ain't nothin' I could put in my field that would give my pesky starlings a worse fright."

"Your wife?" suggested the little voice.

Daisy realised where the voice was coming from. She snatched the scarecrow off the table and stuffed it back in its box.

"Great competition," she stammered. "We should probably be off now."

But she was too late. A little boy at the Whack-a-Mole stand was pointing at the cardboard box. "I saw it with my own eyes!" he shouted. "That scarecrow's lips were moving!"

CHAPTER 5

Daisy dashed across the village green with the cardboard box under her arm and Libby close behind her.

"Our scarecrow wasn't made by a pixie," Daisy panted. "Our scarecrow IS a pixie!"

As if to confirm her conclusion, the cheeky voice piped up again inside the box. "Did you see that farmer's nose?" it jabbered. "With a nose that big, you could smell the flowers all the way over in Plymouth! Or you could lie down and use it as a sundial."

"Don't be rude!" hissed Daisy. She reached her BMX and shoved the box into her bike basket.

"Wait!" The little boy who had blown their cover was sprinting across the green to catch them up. "You have to go back to the tent and collect your rosette."

"What?" Daisy stared at him. "There's no way those judges awarded me a rosette after what just happened."

"It's fine, look!" The boy pointed towards the tea tent. "Farmer Seb and the vicar are laughing about it."

Libby and Daisy squinted across the village green, shielding their eyes from the sun. "They're not laughing," said Libby. "They're looking incredibly cross and offended. Farmer Seb's ears have gone bright red, see?"

"You're right," said the boy. "They're furious, and you didn't win a thing."

"So why did you say we did?"

The boy held up a five-pound note.

"Somebody paid me to come over here and distract you."

The girls whirled round, but it was too late.

Daisy's bike basket was empty.

An engine revved nearby and a red car sped away, its back tyres flicking pieces of gravel into the air. Daisy caught a glimpse of the driver's straggly beard, and of the cardboard box on the seat beside him.

"Hey, come back!" yelled Daisy. "That's our pixie!"

The girls jumped on their bikes and pedalled hard to the main road by St Winifred's church.

"Which way did he go?" asked Libby.

"No idea."

They listened hard for a car engine, but all they could hear was the jingling and whooping of Morris dancers on the village green behind them.

Daisy felt tears pricking the corners of her eyes. That strange, mischievous pixie had ridden a Dartmoor pony to their house and had spent all night in her room, working on two amazing flower arrangements. It had even disguised itself as a scarecrow, just for a laugh. But thanks to her carelessness, that extraordinary creature was now a prisoner of Mr Butchart.

"It's gone for ever, isn't it?" she said out loud.

"Don't be so sure," said Libby. She had jumped off her bike and was standing at the village notice board, keying the No More Moles number into her phone.

"Hello, Mr Butchart," said Libby briskly. "I think you have something that doesn't belong to you, and if you're not back here in three minutes, we're telling the police."

"What did he say?" asked Daisy, as her sister pocketed the phone.

"He said he's going to auction the pixie to the highest bidder and get stinking rich. And he says we're welcome to go to the police because they'll never believe us."

"So why are you smiling?"

"Because I know exactly where he is. I heard a waterfall in the background, and the rattle of his car going over a cattle grid."

"Becky Falls!" cried Daisy.

"That's right." Libby jumped back on her bike. "Come on!"

They raced down the hill past Rose Cottage and the Kestor Inn, past dry-stone walls and telegraph poles, past hedgerows thick with primroses and celandine.

The road levelled out at the bottom as it entered Becca Woods. The girls juddered over the cattle grid and across an ancient stone bridge with the brook babbling beneath. As they rounded a corner in the road, they came across an unexpected sight: six woolly-headed alpacas standing in the road.

The gate to the Becky Falls animal sanctuary had been knocked clean off its hinges, and the fence of the alpaca pen lay in splinters on the ground.

Using a plank of wood as a ramp, Libby and Daisy soared over the debris and landed in the field beyond, still peddling hard. The tyre marks of the mole catcher's car were clear to see, and the girls were hot on his tail. They jumped another shattered fence, and slogged their way uphill through the forest, past limpid pools and tumbling waterfalls.

"Look!" Daisy pointed to the other side of the brook. "Butchart's car has crashed!"

"There are stepping stones ahead!" called Libby. "How are your bunny hops these days?"

"Better than yours," laughed Daisy.

They crossed the stepping stones in a series of rapid jumps, then stood up tall in their saddles and powered up the far bank, which was carpeted with sun-dappled bluebells.

The mole catcher's car had smacked head-on into a silver birch tree. Smoke rose from the crumpled bonnet and the driver's door stood open.

"He's on foot now!" cried Libby. "We've got the advantage!"

They rode up a footpath, through a muddy puddle and out onto open moorland. This area was known as Hound Tor Marshes, and Mum and Dad were always warning them about it. *One false step, girls, and you'll disappear into the slurping bog, never to be seen again.*

Mr Butchart was right there in front of them, and he had already taken more than one false step. He was sinking further with every movement, yet still he blundered forward.

Libby and Daisy rode up over the bridleway and came down onto a patch of stony ground a few yards from the hapless mole catcher.

"Stop moving!" Libby yelled. "You're making it worse!"

"Nonsense!" Mr Butchart waved the chuckling pixie high above his head. "I'm on my way to London, where this little fellow will make my fortune!"

"This isn't the way to London!" called Daisy. "You're being pixie led!"

At the words 'pixie led', Mr Butchart seemed to come to his senses. "By Jupiter, you're right!" he said, his cheeks turning suddenly pale. "This imp has proper done me in. Crashed my car, and everything!"

"Take off your jacket, and turn it inside out," said Libby. "It will break the spell."

"I can't do that!" Mr Butchart yelled. "I'm not letting go of the imp!"

The pixie giggled and clapped its tiny hands.

"Mr Butchart, you need to choose!" cried Libby. "Drown with the pixie or survive without it!"

The bog was up to Mr Butchart's waist, sucking and slurping.

"Choose!" screamed Daisy.

Mr Butchart looked down at the bog and his will crumbled in an instant. He put the pixie down on the bog grass, whipped off his jacket and turned it inside-out.

The pixie gave an elaborate bow and scampered off in the direction of Haytor. Daisy could have sworn it gave her a little thumbs-up sign as it sprinted away.

The mole catcher shifted his weight onto his tummy and wriggled across the bog towards the safety of the stony ground. Libby and Daisy grabbed one hand each and pulled him to safety.

"Thank you," gasped the frightened man. "If you two hadn't arrived when you did, I dread to think what might have happened. I was crazy to imagine I could have made my fortune out of that nasty little imp."

"He's not nasty," said Daisy. "Just mischievous. Relations between pixies and humans are never straightforward, Mr Butchart. I'd stick to moles if I were you."

*

By the time Libby and Daisy got back to the village fête, the Morris dancers had finished hopping and every cake in the tea tent had been devoured. They found Mum and Dad sitting on a grassy knoll, sharing an ice-cream in the afternoon sun.

"There you are, girls!" Mum exclaimed. "Daisy, what's this I hear about you being rude to the vicar?"

Daisy was not surprised that her parents had already heard the vicar's side of the story. She knew how quickly gossip travels in small villages, especially in Manaton.

"It's a long story," said Daisy.

"You can write him a letter of apology," said Dad. "And when you've done that, you can write me a letter of congratulation!"

Dad leapt to his feet and unzipped his fleecy jacket to reveal a large, purple rosette in the middle of his chest.

BEETROOT
BEST IN SHOW
MANATON

"Best in show!" Dad gloated. "We'll remember this year's fête for many years to come, girls!"

Libby and Daisy exchanged a secret smile.

"Yes," said Daisy. "Yes, I'm sure we will."

READING ZONE!

QUIZ TIME

Can you remember the answers
to these questions?

1. What name do Libby and Daisy
give Haytor Quarry?

2. What does 'pixie led' mean?

3. What was in the cab of Farmer
Seb's tractor at the fête?

4. Why was the boy paid five pounds
to distract Libby and Daisy?

5. How did the girls know where to
find Mr Butchart after the phonecall?

READING ZONE!

WHAT DO YOU THINK?

In the story the girls are quick to realise what is happening to them when they got lost – the characters in the story seem comfortable with the idea of pixies. Do you believe pixies might exist? Why do you think the stories began in the first place?

READING ZONE!

STORYTELLING TOOLKIT

This book has two parallel stories –
one about Mum and Dad and the other
about the girls. We mostly follow what
happens to the girls and find out
what happened to Mum and Dad
at the end. Do you
think this works
well? Have you
read other books
written like this?

READING ZONE!

GET CREATIVE

Daisy wants to create entries for the fête including a miniature scarecrow, a garden on a dinner plate and a flower arrangement in a thimble. Why not draw a picture of what you would make for fête? You could add labels to say what each part is.

Look out for more books in the
BLOOMSBURY READERS SERIES

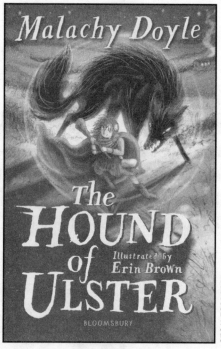

Malachy Doyle

The
HOUND
of
ULSTER

Illustrated by
Erin Brown

BLOOMSBURY

9781447298963

Young Setanta dreams of becoming a champion
warrior but his parents are shepherds and the king's
young warriors are determined to keep Setanta in
his place. To make things worse, that's not the only
obstacle – there's a ferocious hound in the way too...